Don't
Be Afraid,
Little One

FOR ALISON LOWE
WITH LOVE
~C.P.

FOR JULIA AND VICKY
WITH LOVE
~J.C.

This edition produced 2003
for The Travelling Book Company
Troubadour Limited, Express House, Crow Arch Lane,
Ringwood, Hampshire BH24 1PD, by
LITTLE TIGER PRESS
An imprint of Magi Publications,
1 The Coda Centre, 189 Munster Road, London SW6 6AW
www.littletigerpress.com
First published in Great Britain 1998

Text copyright © Caroline Pitcher 1998
Illustrations copyright © Jane Chapman 1998
The author and illustrator have asserted their moral rights
CIP Data is available

Printed in Dubai
1 85430 946 3

1 3 5 7 9 10 8 6 4 2

Don't
Be Afraid,
Little One

CAROLINE PITCHER

ILLUSTRATED BY
JANE CHAPMAN

THE TRAVELLING BOOK COMPANY

One moonlit night, while the wind
raged and the rain drummed on the
stable roof, a mare had her foal.
She breathed on him softly, until he
struggled up on a tangle of long legs.

"What's that noise?" asked the foal.
"Just the wind," said the mare and
nuzzled his velvety neck.
"Where is the wind?"
"It's raging round the hills," replied
his mother. "When you are big and
your legs aren't wobbly anymore,
you will run with the wind over
the hills."
"Will you be there with me?" asked
the foal.
"No," said his mother. "But you
won't think of *me* at all."

The foal didn't like his mother saying that. "Why won't I think of you?" he asked. His mother sighed and shook her long black mane. "Because you won't need me then. Now settle down, little one. No more questions." "What are questions?" yawned the foal, and then he fell fast asleep while the wind raged all around, and the rain drummed on the stable roof.

Spring came, and the foal's legs
grew longer and stronger, so that
his head just reached the top of
the stable door.
"What's outside?" he asked.
"It's a field," said the mare. "Soon
you will be able to go there with
me and run all the way round
and back again."
"I don't think I want to," said
the foal, drawing back. "I don't
like Outside. I like it here."

The foal's legs grew even
stronger and longer. Now he
could see right over the stable
door. He saw other horses.
There was a great shire horse with
hooves as big as rocks, and a tiny
Shetland with very long hair. He saw
a horse as dark as the night sky, and a
pony as pale as moonlight.
"Where are their mothers?" he asked.
"Some of them are here and some are at
other stables," said the mare. "They give
people rides. I'll do that again soon, too,
little one, while you stay behind."
Stay behind!

"No," said the foal, turning his back.
"I don't want to think about it."

When the days grew warmer,
the mare and her foal went out
into the field. They ran all the
way around it and back again.

Twilight fell, and the foal looked uneasy.
"Can't we go back to the stable now?" he asked.
"No," said his mother. "When the nights are
warm, we stay outside."
"But it's *dark!*"
"It's dark in the stable, too, little one. It's the same dark."
"It's not such a big dark," said the foal. "I can't see you out
here when you move away from me. I'm all alone."
"You know I'm here, even if you can't see me,"
whispered the mare.

The foal lifted his head out of the darkness.
"What's making that noise?" he asked.
"Just the wind. Don't you remember
hearing it when you were very small?"
"Yes," said the foal. "But where is it?"
"You know it's there, but you can't see it."
"Just like you in the dark, Mum," he
whispered.

One morning, the foal woke late. He had done so much running and growing the day before he was very tired. *But where was his mother?* The foal looked inside the stable, but she wasn't there. Then he saw her by the fence. She had a bridle over her head and a saddle on her back. "I'm going back to work," she called to him. "I'm going to give rides again."

"And who will ride me?" cried the foal with excitement.

"You're too little to be ridden yet," explained his mother. "Your back is weak, your mouth is soft as silk, and your legs would snap like twigs."

"But I'll be all alone," he wailed. "Oh, please stay with me!"

"No," said the mare, as a little girl climbed
on to her back. "You'll be all right. You won't
think of me at all."
The foal watched as his mother and her
rider trotted out of sight. He was all alone.
"Come back, Mum!" he neighed, and his
voice echoed in the hills.

He heard something answer
him, but it wasn't his mother.
It was the wind!
The wind had come down from the
hills to play with him. It blew in his
mane and his tail, and it blew in the
trees and stirred all the leaves. It blew
a butterfly so that the foal could chase
it, and it blew a path through the
meadow-sweet so that he could run
right through the middle. It even
blew little waves in the water
of his drinking trough.

The foal jumped and ran and
bucked and chased and flicked
his little black tail. He played
with the wind all morning.

And then, just as the foal was too tired to run and jump anymore, his mother came back! She nuzzled his neck and said, "You see – nothing bad happened to you when you were all alone."

Goodness, thought the foal. I didn't think of Mum at all – not once.

"I wasn't alone," he said. "The wind played with me."

"So you didn't think of me at all?"

"Well – er – maybe a *little* bit," said the foal.

"That's good," said the mare. "I was thinking of you all the time!"

More books for you to enjoy from

The Travelling Books Reading Library

The Healthy Wolf
David Bedford & Mandy Stanley

Charlie & Tess
Martin Hall & Catherine Walters

The Great Goat Chase
Tony Bonning & Sally Hobson

George and Sylvia
Michael Coleman & Tim Warnes

It Could Have Been Worse
AH Benjamin & Tim Warnes

The Long Journey Home
David Bedford & Penny Ives

Sleepy Sam
Michael Catchpool & Eleanor Taylor

Titus's Troublesome Tooth
Linda Jennings & Gwyneth Williamson

Davy's Scary Journey
Christine Leeson & Tim Warnes

Clever Little Freddy
Christine Leeson & Joanne Moss

One, Two, Three, Oops!
Michael Coleman & Gwyneth Williamson

Run Little Fawn, Run!
Sheridan Cain & Gavin Rowe

Lazy Ozzie
Michael Coleman & Gwyneth Williamson

Ridiculous!
Michael Coleman & Gwyneth Williamson

TRAVELLING BOOKS
READING LIBRARY